America's Game
Montreal Expos

Chris Sehnert

ABDO & Daughters
PUBLISHING

Published by Abdo & Daughters, 4940 Viking Dr., Suite 622, Edina, MN 55435.

Copyright ©1997 by Abdo Consulting Group, Inc., Pentagon Tower, P.O. Box 36036, Minneapolis, Minnesota 55435. International copyrights reserved in all countries. No part of this book may be reproduced in any form without written permission from the publisher. Printed in the United States.

Cover photo: Allsport

Interior photos: Wide World Photo, pages 1, 5, 7, 8, 10-12, 15, 16, 22-27.

Edited by Paul Joseph

Library of Congress Cataloging–in–Publication Data

Sehnert, Chris W.
   Montreal Expos / Chris Sehnert
      p. cm. — (America's game)
   Includes index.
   Summary: A history of the Montreal Expos, the team that brought big-league baseball to Canada, as members of the National League East.
   ISBN 1-56239-675-7
   1. Montreal Expos (Baseball team)—Juvenile literature.
[1. Montreal Expos (Baseball team)—History 2. Baseball—History.]
I. Title. II. Series.
GV875.M6S45 1997
796.357'64'09714281—dc20   96-25684
                                          CIP

Contents

Montreal Expos 4

The Great Expansion 6

First And Worst Season 7

"Le Grande Orange" 9

The Race Is On! 10

Let The Sunshine In! 12

Carter, Dawson, And Parrish 14

The Team Of The '80s? 16

One Game Away 20

Expos Stars Come And Go 22

Building For Other Teams 24

A Championship Season? 28

Glossary 29

Index 31

Montreal Expos

Over the years, Montreal, Quebec, has come to be known for its international appeal. It is home to more French-speaking people than any city, other than Paris, France. Two years before Major League Baseball arrived in Canada, Montreal hosted the World's Fair. The event attracted 50 million visitors, and was called "Expo '67." In 1969, the city's new ballclub was named the Montreal Expos.

Baseball was not an entirely new game for the people of Montreal. The top minor league team in the Brooklyn Dodgers' farm system had been the Montreal Royals. Jackie Robinson played the 1946 season with the Royals. He became the first African-American player in the minor leagues, one year before he integrated the majors.

Facing page: Montreal Expos' manager Felipe Alou gives some pointers to his son, outfielder Moises Alou, while watching a game during spring training in 1996.

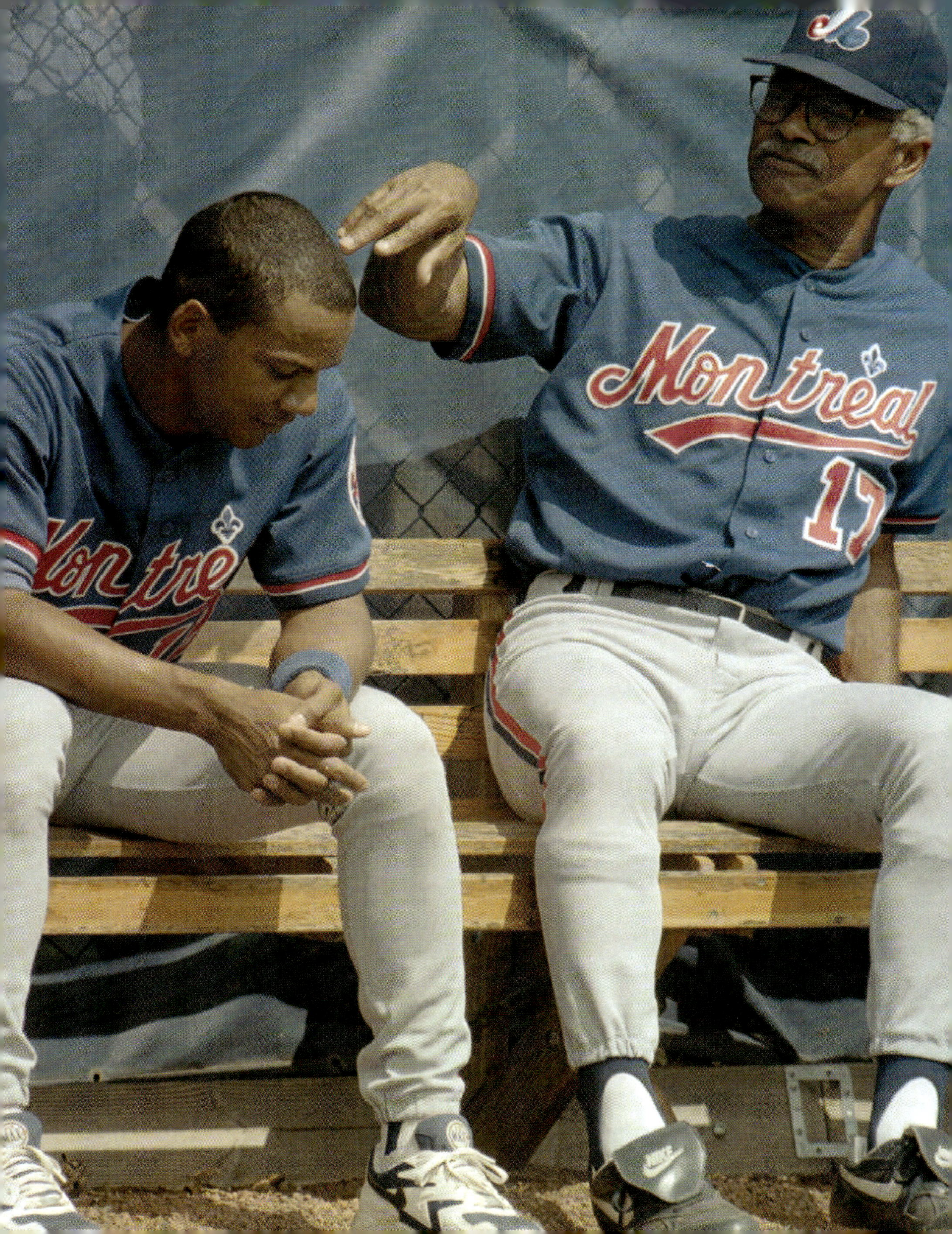
Montreal
17
NIKE

The Great Expansion

The Montreal Expos were part of Major League Baseball's great expansion of the 1960s. The Washington Senators, Los Angeles Angels, Houston Colt .45s, and New York Mets had all been added earlier in the decade. In 1969, the Kansas City Royals, Seattle Pilots, San Diego Padres, and Montreal Expos rounded out the great expansion.

With 12 teams in each league, divisional play was set up to enhance competition. In the National League (NL), the Padres became California's fifth major league franchise, and joined the NL West. The Montreal Expos brought big-league baseball to Canada as members of the NL East.

Without exception, major league expansion teams have struggled in their first years. The New York Mets provided hope for baseball's newest members in 1969, winning the World Series in only their eighth season of play. The Kansas City Royals (1985) and Toronto Blue Jays (1992 and 1993) have also come from expansion to win the World Championship. The Montreal Expos are among the handful of teams who have yet to reach top status.

First And Worst Season

The Expos' first season got off to a rousing start when pitcher Bill Stoneman threw a no-hitter in their ninth game. Montreal defeated the Philadelphia Phillies (7-0). It turned out to be one of the few highlights in the Expos' worst season on record (52-110). They finished 48 games out of first place, on the bottom of the NL East.

Jose "Coco" Laboy and Mack "The Knife" Jones powered the Expos' offense in their inaugural season. They combined for 40 home runs (HRs) and 162 runs batted in (RBIs). Unfortunately, Coco and the Knife were never able to match that level of output again. Both were eventually benched for a lack of defensive ability.

Expos' pitcher Bill Stoneman in 1971.

"Le Grande Orange," Expos' All-Star slugger Rusty Staub.

"Le Grande Orange"

Daniel "Rusty" Staub was a fan favorite for the Expos in the early years. The red-headed Cajun was nicknamed "Le Grande Orange" by the French-Canadian fans. Staub began his career with the expansion Colt .45s. In 1967, the same year the Colt .45s were renamed the Houston Astros, Staub became an NL All-Star. He led the NL in doubles (44), while posting the highest batting average of his 23-year major league career (.333).

In three seasons with the Montreal Expos, Rusty nailed 78 home runs. He was an NL All-Star in all three seasons (1969-1971).

Carl Morton became the ace of the Expos' pitching staff in their second season. He picked up 18 wins on his way to becoming the 1970 NL Rookie of the Year. Montreal improved their record by 21 games (73-89) that season, but remained on the bottom of the NL East. In 1971, they would pass the Philadelphia Phillies to finish out of the cellar for the first time.

Rusty Staub became known as the most popular athlete in Canada who did not wear skates. When he was traded to the New York Mets before the 1972 season, Expos fans were in shock. Staub went on to become the only player who has collected 500 hits with four different ballclubs. He retired after the 1985 season with 2,716 career hits and 1,466 RBIs. The Montreal Expos retired the uniform number 10 of "Le Grande Orange" in 1992.

Steve Rogers delivers a pitch in a 1976 game against the New York Mets.

The Race Is On!

The Montreal Expos rose to respectability quicker than most expansion franchises. Their counterparts in the NL West, the San Diego Padres, finished in last place six straight times. The Expos moved out of the NL East's basement in their third season. By their fifth season Montreal had become a legitimate contender.

In 1973, the NL East division title was up for grabs. Top-to-bottom it was the closest race in the history of the major leagues. By late August, only six games separated the first place St. Louis Cardinals from the last place New York Mets. The Pittsburgh Pirates took over the lead with just weeks to go in the season. With a six-game winning streak, the Montreal Expos caught the Pirates in mid-September.

Helping the Expos to their finest season yet was rookie right-hander Steve Rogers. He won 10 of his 17 starting assignments on his way to posting a sparkling 1.54 ERA (earned run average). Rogers finished just behind San Francisco Giants' outfielder Gary Matthews in the 1973 NL Rookie of the Year voting.

Mike Marshall was in his fourth season with the Expos in 1973. "Iron Mike" led NL relief pitchers in saves with 31, and set a major league record for appearances with 92. The next season Marshall broke his own record, appearing in 106 games for the Los Angeles Dodgers. He won the 1974 NL Cy Young Award, after being traded by the Expos.

Ken Singleton arrived in Montreal in 1972. He was part of the unpopular trade that had sent Rusty Staub to the Mets. Singleton's bat kindled the Expos' offense during their 1973 pennant chase. He had the league's highest on-base percentage (.429), and became the first Montreal player to record 100 RBIs in a season, with 103.

The six-game winning streak that vaulted Montreal into the penthouse of the NL East was immediately followed by disappointment. The Expos dropped 9 of the next 10 games, crushing all hope of a championship season. The New York Mets rallied from last place to win their second NL East division title. Montreal finished in fourth place, just 3.5 games back.

Expos' outfielder Ken Singleton in 1982.

Let The Sunshine In!

In 1974, Montreal finished fourth in the NL East for the second straight time. The following season they began a downward trend. By 1976, the team had returned to the division's basement, finishing

46 games behind the Philadelphia Phillies. That summer, the International Olympic Games were held in Montreal. Olympic Stadium was built to host the world-class athletic competitions. The next year it became the new home of the Montreal Expos.

The Expos played their first eight seasons in an old minor league facility. Even with its tiny seating capacity (under 30,000), Montreal consistently drew more than the major league average of fans per season. But then in 1975, when the team began to drop off in the standings, their attendance dropped below one million fans for the first time. In 1977, a new crop of young players moved into Montreal's brand new ballpark, and the Expos began rising in the East once again.

Olympic Stadium was originally designed to have the first retractable roof. The plans called for a lid that would open to let the sunshine in, and close to keep out the cold and rain. The project was left incomplete, leaving a giant hole in the stadium's ceiling. When the roof at "The Big O" was finally completed in 1988, its retractable nature was rarely functional.

The sun is bound to shine on the Montreal Expos someday. It won't be through the roof of "The Big O," however. When a beam weighing 55 tons fell from the structure in September 1991, the team was forced to play their remaining schedule on the road. Since then the roof has been permanently closed.

Facing page: Montreal's Olympic Stadium in 1980, before the retractable roof was installed.

Carter, Dawson, And Parrish

In 1975, Gary Carter was an outstanding rookie outfielder for the Expos. In 1977, he took over as Montreal's full-time catcher. Carter went on to win the NL Gold Glove Award three straight times (1980-1982). His 31 home runs in 1977 paced the Expos' turnaround.

A 22-year old outfielder named Andre Dawson began his career with the Montreal Expos in 1977. He led the team with 21 stolen bases, and set an Expo rookie record, smashing 19 homers. Dawson became the second Montreal player to win the NL Rookie of the Year Award.

Montreal moved up a notch to fourth place in 1978. Veteran left-hander Ross Grimsley joined the team that year. The bearded southpaw became the first Expos pitcher to reach 20 wins in a single season (20-11).

In 1979, Bill "Spaceman" Lee helped rocket the Expos to their finest season (95-65). Lee combined with Grimsley, Steve Rogers, and Dan Schatzeder to give Montreal the NL's best pitching staff. Montreal's hurlers allowed the fewest walks (450), fewest runs (581), and had the league's lowest ERA (3.14).

On offense, Larry Parrish set the pace with a .307 batting average. He backed up the Philadelphia Phillies' Mike Schmidt as the NL's

All-Star third baseman that season. Parrish (30), Dawson (25), and Carter (22) smacked a total of 77 homers for the Expos in 1979.

The race for the 1979 NL East Division title was a two-team affair. The Pittsburgh Pirates and Montreal Expos battled down the stretch. On September 18, the two teams met in a six-hour rain-drenched marathon. Willie Stargell's 11th-inning homer gave the Pirates a crucial victory. Gary Carter injured his thumb in the last week of the season. Without Carter in the lineup, the Expos lost four of their last five games. They finished in second place, just two games behind Pittsburgh.

In 1980, Montreal was involved in another fight to the finish. On the season's final weekend the Philadelphia Phillies entered Olympic Stadium in a first-place tie with the Expos. For the second-straight season, a future Hall-of-Famer defeated Montreal with an 11th-inning blast. Mike Schmidt put the Phillies ahead to stay, and the Expos finished one game back.

Gary Carter is called safe at home during a 1979 game against the Philadelphia Phillies.

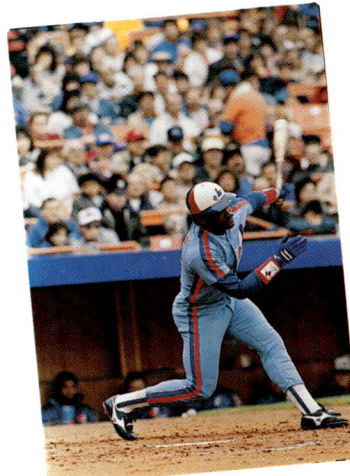

Outfielder Tim Raines hits a home run in a 1987 game against the New York Mets.

The Team Of The '80s?

After Montreal's near misses in 1979 and 1980, many baseball experts predicted the Expos would be the "Team of the '80s." Their predictions were bolstered in 1981 by rookie outfielder Tim Raines. Raines would become one of the greatest base-stealers of all time.

The 1981 Major League Baseball season was the only season in which having the best record did not qualify a team for the playoffs. In the NL West, the Cincinnati Reds won more ball games (66) than any team in baseball. But the Los Angeles Dodgers (63 wins) won the NL West Division title. The St. Louis Cardinals had the best winning percentage (59-43) in the NL East. They, too, were left out of the post-season. In one of baseball's strangest seasons, the Montreal Expos won their only NL East Division title.

By early June, with the Expos holding on to third place in their division, the season came to an abrupt standstill. Negotiations between representatives of the players and owners over a new labor contract had stalled. Without a basic agreement, the players went on strike.

Play resumed in August under a split-season format. The unusual plan was suggested by Commissioner Bowie Kuhn. It called for the winners of the season's "first half" to meet the leaders from the "second half" in a mini-playoff to determine divisional champions.

When the season's second half got underway, the Montreal Expos had 53 games remaining on their schedule. The St. Louis Cardinals had 52 games left. Taking full advantage of the scheduling quirk, the Expos picked up 30 victories to become the NL East's second-half champions. The Cardinals won 29 of their remaining contests to finish second by half a game.

The Philadelphia Phillies had won the most games in the first half of the season. They met the Montreal Expos in the divisional championship series. The Phillies' ace pitcher was future Hall-of-Famer Steve "Lefty" Carlton.

Tim "Rock" Raines was Montreal's new lead-off hitter in 1981. In his rookie season, Raines had 71 stolen bases to lead the NL. He finished second in the 1981 NL Rookie of the Year balloting, behind the Los Angeles Dodgers' pitching sensation, Fernando Valenzuela.

The Expos and Phillies hooked up for a pitchers' duel in Game 1 of their best-of-five playoff. Montreal scored three runs off Lefty Carlton, and a solid performance by veteran Steve Rogers preserved the 3-1 victory. The next day, a two-run homer by Gary Carter put the Expos one win away from their first division championship.

With victories in Game 3 and Game 4, the Phillies tied the series (2-2), forcing a critical final meeting. Game 5 was a rematch of staff aces. For the second time in five days, the Expos defeated Steve Carlton. Steve Rogers' two-run single was the crucial hit, as he shutout Philadelphia 3-0, and sent the Montreal Expos to their first National League Championship Series (NLCS).

Montreal

Daniel "Rusty" Staub was an NL All-Star in all three seasons with the Expos (1969-1971).

In his 1973 rookie season, Steve Rogers posted a 1.54 ERA, and finished second in Rookie of the Year voting.

In 1973, Ken Singleton became the first Montreal player to record 100 RBIs in a season, with 103.

Gary Carter won the NL Gold Glove Award three straight times (1980-1982).

Expos

With 71 stolen bases in 1981, Tim Raines finished second in NL Rookie of the Year balloting.

Al Oliver led the NL in hits (204), doubles (43), and RBIs (109) in 1982. He was the NL's batting champion in his first season with the Expos.

Andres Galarraga won the NL's Gold Glove Award in 1989 and 1990.

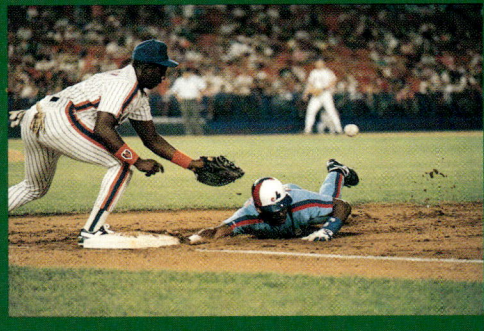

Marquis Grissom led the NL in stolen bases in 1991 and 1992.

One Game Away

The Expos were attempting to become the first Canadian team to make it to the World Series. They would have to defeat the Los Angeles Dodgers to get there. The 1981 NLCS was another best-of-five series. Once again it would take all five games to determine a champion.

The series opened in Los Angeles, where the Dodgers defeated Bill Gullickson to win Game 1. The following afternoon, the Expos faced the 1981 NL Cy Young Award winner, Fernando Valenzuela. Montreal countered with Ray Burris. Burris silenced "Fernando-Mania" with a five-hit shutout, leading the Expos to victory.

The series moved to Olympic Stadium for Game 3, where the Expos' Steve Rogers picked up his third-straight post-season victory (4-1). This time, the Expos were one win away from the NL Pennant. In Game 4, the Dodgers' Steve Garvey smashed an eighth-inning homer. The home run broke a 1-1 tie, and Los Angeles went on to even the series at two games apiece.

The NL's post-season had been dominated by tremendous pitching. The stage was set for one last duel to determine the 1981 NL Champions. Ray Burris and Fernando Valenzuela battled for eight innings to another 1-1 tie. In the ninth inning, Steve Rogers was summoned from the Montreal bullpen one last time. Rogers had allowed a total of two runs in his previous three complete-game efforts. In Game 5 he recorded two outs before yielding Rick Monday's series-winning home run.

The Montreal Expos have never returned to the post-season. They could hardly have come closer to an NL Championship. For the remainder of the decade the Expos finished no higher than third place. The high expectation of being the "Team of the '80s" was never achieved.

Expos Stars Come And Go

Steve Rogers returned to have his finest season in 1982. He led the NL in ERA (2.40) and recorded 19 wins. Rogers placed second in the 1982 NL Cy Young Award balloting.

Al Oliver led the NL in hits (204), doubles (43), and RBIs (109) in 1982. The former Texas Ranger and Pittsburgh Pirate was also the NL's batting champion in his first of two seasons with the Expos!

Al Oliver watches the first of his two home runs during a 1983 game against the Chicago Cubs.

Pete Rose watches the ball as he heads for first during a 1984 game against the Philadelphia Phillies.

Pete Rose began the 1984 season with Montreal. After playing in only 95 games, he returned to end his career in his hometown of Cincinnati. Rose lined his 4,000th hit as a member of the Expos. He retired in 1986 as Major League Baseball's all-time hit king (4,256).

In 1984, Gary Carter led the NL with 106 RBIs. The next season he was traded to the New York Mets. Carter led the Mets to the 1986 World Championship. In 1992, he returned to the Expos to finish his 19-year playing career.

After hitting 225 home runs in 10 seasons with Montreal, Andre Dawson became a Chicago Cub in 1987. He was the NL's MVP (Most Valuable Player) in his first season away from Montreal. Dawson, along with Willie Mays, Bobby Bonds, and Barry Bonds are the only four players in major league history with 300 career home runs and 300 stolen bases.

Tim Raines made seven-straight All-Star appearances with the Expos before joining the Chicago White Sox in 1991. Raines led the NL in stolen bases four times, and was the 1986 NL batting champion. He currently ranks fifth on the all-time stolen base list, with 777.

Expos' first baseman Andres Galarraga slides safely into home in a 1988 game against the New York Yankees.

Building For Other Teams

The Montreal Expos have become a virtual breeding ground of superstar major league ballplayers in the 1990s. Unfortunately for their fans, the team has been unable to keep their young talent around long enough to bring home an NL pennant.

Andres Galarraga was an Expos rookie in 1986. Two years later he made his first All-Star appearance, and led the NL in hits (184) and doubles (42). Nicknamed the "Big Cat" for his defensive quickness, Andres became the NL's Gold Glove first baseman in 1989. Galarraga won a second Gold Glove in 1990, before being traded to the St. Louis Cardinals in 1992. He was the NL's batting champion as a member of the Colorado Rockies in 1993.

Hoping to fulfill their "Team of the '80s" destiny before the decade was up, the Expos traded for veteran left-hander Mark Langston in 1989. They sent their 6-foot 10-inch rookie southpaw, Randy Johnson, to the Seattle Mariners to seal the deal.

Langston performed well for the Expos, finishing third in the NL with a 2.39 ERA. Montreal finished in fourth place, 12 games behind the Chicago Cubs. The next year, Langston left as a free agent for the California Angels.

As a Mariner, Randy Johnson has become the most dominating left-hander in all of baseball. "The Big Unit" won the 1995 AL Cy Young Award, and has led the league in strikeouts four-straight times.

Pitcher Mark Langston looks upset after giving up three runs in the first inning during a 1989 game against the San Francisco Giants.

Larry Walker, Marquis Grissom, and Delino DeShields were all members of the Expos who received votes for the 1990 NL Rookie of the Year Award. By 1995, all three had moved on to other teams.

Walker, a native of Canada, had been drafted by the Montreal Canadiens (National Hockey League) to play goalie. He decided to play baseball instead. Walker became the NL's Gold Glove right-fielder in 1992. He signed as a free agent with the Colorado Rockies in 1995, where he finished second in the NL with 36 home runs.

Center fielder Marquis Grissom led the NL in stolen bases in 1991 (76), and 1992 (78). He was traded to the Atlanta Braves in 1995. Grissom won his third-straight Gold Glove Award that season, and helped his new club to its first World Championship.

New York Mets' first baseman Garry Templeton can't catch a wild pick-off throw as Expos' runner Marquis Grissom slides safely back to first base.

Atlanta Braves' baserunner Jim Presley yells as he is tagged hard by Expos' second baseman Delino DeShields.

    Delino DeShields finished second to Atlanta Braves' David Justice in the 1990 NL Rookie of the Year voting. DeShields was traded to the Los Angeles Dodgers in 1994. In return, the Expos received pitcher Pedro "PJ" Martinez.

    Dennis Martinez was Montreal's staff ace from 1986 to 1993. Dennis made three-straight All-Star appearances (1990-1992) while playing for the Expos. Martinez pitched the 15th perfect game in major league history on July 28, 1991. His no-hit and no-walk complete game effort, in which he shut out the Los Angeles Dodgers (2-0), helped Martinez to a league-leading ERA (2.39) that season. At 38 years old, Dennis Martinez signed with the Cleveland Indians in 1994.

A Championship Season?

In 1992, Montreal hired Felipe Alou to manage the ever-changing face of the Expos' lineup. That season, the Toronto Blue Jays became the first Canadian team to win baseball's World Championship. The Montreal Expos are still trying.

Felipe Alou became the first Dominican-born manager. Felipe has kept the Expos competitive, thanks in part to his son Moises Alou, who also joined the team in 1992. Moises finished second in the NL Rookie of the Year voting that year. He is among the latest young stars who have begun their careers in Montreal.

The Montreal Expos have faced a unique problem in the 1990s. They have developed more star players than any single team could possibly afford. With a spring of young talent that continues to flow, Montreal baseball fans are anxiously awaiting a pennant-winning season—better yet, a World Series Championship season.

Glossary

All-Star: A player who is voted by fans as the best player at one position in a given year.

American League (AL): An association of baseball teams formed in 1900 which make up one-half of the major leagues.

American League Championship Series (ALCS): A best-of-seven-game playoff with the winner going to the World Series to face the National League Champions.

Batting Average: A baseball statistic calculated by dividing a batter's hits by the number of times at bat.

Earned Run Average (ERA): A baseball statistic which calculates the average number of runs a pitcher gives up per nine innings of work.

Fielding Average: A baseball statistic which calculates a fielder's success rate based on the number of chances the player has to record an out.

Hall of Fame: A memorial for the greatest baseball players of all time, located in Cooperstown, New York.

Home Run (HR): A play in baseball where a batter hits the ball over the outfield fence scoring everyone on base as well as the batter.

Major Leagues: The highest ranking associations of professional baseball teams in the world, currently consisting of the American and National Baseball Leagues.

Minor Leagues: A system of professional baseball leagues at levels below Major League Baseball.

National League (NL): An association of baseball teams formed in 1876 which make up one-half of the major leagues.

National League Championship Series (NLCS): A best-of-seven-game playoff with the winner going to the World Series to face the American League Champions.

Pennant: A flag which symbolizes the championship of a professional baseball league.

Pitcher: The player on a baseball team who throws the ball for the batter to hit. The pitcher stands on a mound and pitches the ball toward the strike zone area above the plate.

Plate: The place on a baseball field where a player stands to bat. It is used to determine the width of the strike zone. Forming the point of the diamond-shaped field, it is the final goal a base runner must reach to score a run.

RBI: A baseball statistic standing for *runs batted in.* Players receive an RBI for each run that scores on their hits.

Rookie: A first-year player, especially in a professional sport.

Slugging Percentage: A statistic which points out a player's ability to hit for extra bases by taking the number of total bases hit and dividing it by the number of at bats.

Stolen Base: A play in baseball when a base runner advances to the next base while the pitcher is delivering the pitch.

Strikeout: A play in baseball when a batter is called out for failing to put the ball in play after the pitcher has delivered three strikes.

Triple Crown: A rare accomplishment when a single player finishes a season leading their league in batting average, home runs, and RBIs. A pitcher can win a Triple Crown by leading the league in wins, ERA, and strikeouts.

Walk: A play in baseball when a batter receives four pitches out of the strike zone and is allowed to go to first base.

World Series: The championship of Major League Baseball played since 1903 between the pennant winners from the American and National Leagues.

Index

A
Alou, Felipe 28
Alou, Moises 28
Atlanta Braves 26

B
Bonds, Barry 23
Bonds, Bobby 23
Brooklyn Dodgers 4
Burris, Ray 20, 21

C
California Angels 25
Carlton, Steve "Lefty" 17
Carter, Gary 14, 15, 17, 23
Chicago Cubs 25
Chicago White Sox 23
Cincinnati Reds 16
Cleveland Indians 27
Colorado Rockies 24, 26
Cy Young Award 11, 20, 22, 25

D
Dawson, Andre 14, 15, 23
DeShields, Delino 26, 27
Dominican Republic 28

G
Galarraga, Andres 24
Garvey, Steve 21
Gold Glove Award 14, 24, 26
Grimsley, Ross 14
Grissom, Marquis 26
Gullickson, Bill 20

H
Houston Colt .45s 6

I
International Olympic Games 13

J
Johnson, Randy 25
Jones, Mack "The Knife" 7
Justice, David 27

K
Kansas City Royals 6
Kuhn, Bowie 17

L
Laboy, Jose "Coco" 7
Langston, Mark 25
Lee, Bill "Spaceman" 14
Los Angeles Angels 6
Los Angeles Dodgers 11, 16, 20, 27

M
Marshall, Mike 11
Martinez, Dennis 27

Martinez, Pedro "PJ" 27
Matthews, Gary 10
Mays, Willie 23
Montreal Canadiens 26
Montreal Royals 4
Morton, Carl 9

N

National League (NL) 6, 7, 9-12, 14-17, 20-28
National League Championship Series (NLCS) 17, 20
New York Mets 6, 9, 10, 11, 23

O

Oliver, Al 22
Olympic Stadium 13, 15, 21

P

Paris, France 4
Parrish, Larry 14, 15
Philadelphia Phillies 7, 9, 13, 15, 17
Pittsburgh Pirates 10, 15

R

Raines, Tim 16, 17, 23
Robinson, Jackie 4
Rogers, Steve 10, 14, 17, 21, 22
Rookie of the Year 9, 10, 14, 17, 26, 27, 28
Rose, Pete 23

S

San Diego Padres 6, 10
Schatzeder, Dan 14
Schmidt, Mike 14, 15
Seattle Pilots 6
Singleton, Ken 11
St. Louis Cardinals 10, 16, 17, 24
Stargell, Willie 15
Staub, Daniel "Rusty" 9, 11
Stoneman, Bill 7

T

Toronto Blue Jays 6, 28

V

Valenzuela, Fernando 17, 20, 21

W

Walker, Larry 26
Washington Senators 6
World Series 6, 20, 28